PowerKids Readers:

The Bilingual Library of the
United States of America

Bilingual Edition
English/Spanish
Edición bilingüe

DISTRICT
OF COLUMBIA

DISTRITO
DE COLUMBIA

VANESSA BROWN

TRADUCCIÓN AL ESPAÑOL: MARÍA CRISTINA BRUSCA

The Rosen Publishing Group's
PowerKids Press™ & **Editorial Buenas Letras**™
New York

Published in 2005 by The Rosen Publishing Group, Inc.
29 East 21st Street, New York, NY 10010

First Edition

Book Layout Design: Thomas Somers
Photo Credits: Cover © Dean Conger/Corbis; p. 5 © Michelle Innes; p.5 (inset) © One Mile Up, Inc.; p. 7 © Galen Rowell/Corbis; p.11© Taylor S. Kennedy/National Geographic Image Collection; p.13 © Museum of the City of New York/Corbis; pp.15, 30 (founding date) © Corbis; p.15 (inset) Detail from Cox Corridoors, U.S. Capitol, Architect of the Capiitol; p.17 © Corbis; pp.19, 31 (Congress) © Wally McNamee/Corbis; p.21© Lee Snider/Photo Images/Corbis; p.23 © Reuters/Corbis; pp. 25,30 (Capital City) © Free Agents Limited/Corbis; p. 30 (American beauty) © Gerrit Greve/Corbis, p. 30 (Wood thrush) © Joe McDonald/Corbis, p.30 (Scarlet oak) © Altrendo/Getty Images; p. 31 (Wilson, Ellington, Slavery) © Bettmann/Corbis; p. 31 (Scalia) © Brooks Kraft/Corbis; p. 31 (Gaye) © Neal Preston/Corbis; p. 31 (Jackson) © Frank Trapper/Corbis; p. 31 (Hawn) © Mitchell Gerber/Corbis; p. 31(Supreme Court) © Joseph Sohm; ChromoSohm Inc./Corbis.

Library of Congress Cataloging-in-Publication Data

Brown, Vanessa, 1963–
Washington, D.C. / Vanessa Brown ; traducción al español, María Cristina Brusca.— 1st ed.
p. cm. — (The bilingual library of the United States of America) Includes bibliographical references and index. ISBN 1-4042-3072-6 (library binding)
1. Washington (D.C.)—Juvenile literature. I. Title. II. Series.

F194.3.B76 2005
975.3—dc22

2005001245

Manufactured in the United States of America

Due to the changing nature of Internet links, Editorial Buenas Letras has developed an online list of Web sites related to the subject of this book. This site is updated regularly. Please use this link to access the list:

http://www.buenasletraslinks.com/ls/dc

Contents

Contenido

Welcome to the District of Columbia

Washington, D.C., is the capital of the United States of America.
Washington, D.C., is also known as the District of Columbia.

Bienvenidos al Distrito de Columbia

Washington, D.C. es la capital de los Estados Unidos de América. Washington, D.C. también es conocida como el Distrito de Columbia.

The Flag and Seal of the District of Columbia

Bandera y escudo del Distrito de Columbia

Washington, D.C., is the only city in the United States that does not belong to a state. The District of Columbia is the home of the U.S. federal government.

Washington, D.C. es la única ciudad de los Estados Unidos que no pertenece a un estado. El Distrito de Columbia es la sede del gobierno federal de los Estados Unidos.

The White House, Home of the U.S. President

La Casa Blanca, hogar del Presidente de E.U.A.

The District of Columbia Geography

The District of Columbia borders the states of Maryland and Virginia. The Potomac River runs on the western border.

Geografía del Distrito de Columbia

El Distrito de Columbia linda con los estados de Maryland y Virginia. El río Potomac corre sobre la frontera oeste.

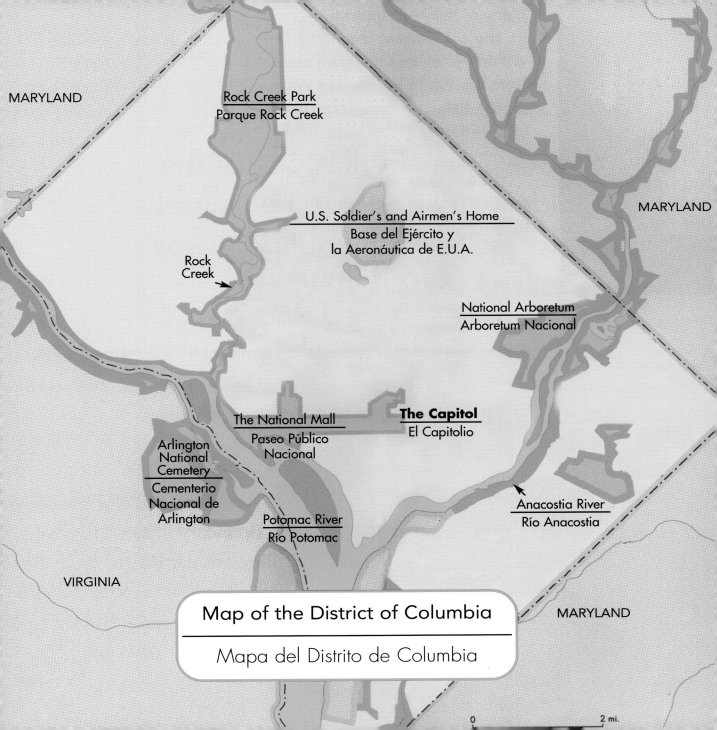

MARYLAND

Rock Creek Park
Parque Rock Creek

MARYLAND

U.S. Soldier's and Airmen's Home
Base del Ejército y
la Aeronáutica de E.U.A.

Rock
Creek

National Arboretum
Arboretum Nacional

The Capitol
El Capitolio

The National Mall
Paseo Público
Nacional

Arlington
National
Cemetery
Cementerio
Nacional de
Arlington

Anacostia River
Río Anacostia

Potomac River
Río Potomac

VIRGINIA

MARYLAND

Map of the District of Columbia

Mapa del Distrito de Columbia

0   2 mi.

Rock Creek Park is one of the oldest city parks in the United States. This national park was built in 1890.

El Parque Rock Creek es uno de los parques más antiguos de los Estados Unidos. Este parque nacional se creó en 1890.

A View of Rock Creek Park

Una vista del Parque Rock Creek

The District of Columbia History

Washington, D.C., became the U.S. capital in 1800. George Washington was the first president of the United States. He chose the land where the city was built. The city was named after him.

Historia del Distrito de Columbia

Washington, D.C. es la capital de E.U.A. desde el año 1800. El primer presidente de los Estados Unidos fue George Washington. El escogió el terreno donde se construyó la ciudad. La ciudad fue nombrada en su honor.

George Washington

Pierre Charles L'Enfant planned Washington, D.C. L'Enfant wanted to build a city with wide avenues and streets. He wanted the streets centered around the governmental buildings.

Pierre Charles L'Enfant planeó Washington, D.C. L'Enfant deseaba construir una ciudad de calles y avenidas anchas. L'Enfant quería que las calles rodearan los edificios del gobierno.

A Plan of the Streets of Washington, D.C., 1794

Plano de las calles de Washington, D.C., 1794

Pierre Charles L'Enfant

Frederick Douglass fought against slavery. In the 1800s, black people did not have freedom. Douglass worked with President Abraham Lincoln in Washington D.C. to write the rules that freed black slaves.

Frederick Douglass luchó contra la esclavitud. En los años 1800, las personas negras no eran libres. Douglass trabajó junto al presidente Abraham Lincoln en Washington D.C. escribiendo las leyes que liberaron a los esclavos.

Frederick Douglass

Living in the District of Columbia

Most people in the District of Columbia work for the U.S. government. The president, the judges of the Supreme Court, and the members of Congress all work in Washington, D.C.

La vida en el Distrito de Columbia

La mayoría de la gente que vive en el Distrito de Columbia trabaja para el gobierno de E.U.A. En Washington, D.C. trabajan el Presidente, los jueces de la Corte Suprema y los miembros del Congreso.

The U.S. Senate

El Senado de E.U.A.

Not everything in Washington, D.C., has to do with government. The city has many important museums. The Smithsonian Institution is the largest group of museums in the world.

No todo, en Washington, D.C., está relacionado con el gobierno. La ciudad tiene muchos museos importantes. La Institución Smithsonian es el grupo más grande de museos del mundo.

The Smithsonian Museum

El Museo Smithsonian

Washington, D.C., is a fun city to live in or visit. The city has many events like the White House Easter Egg Roll. Every spring thousands of kids visit the White House to hunt for Easter eggs!

Vivir o visitar Washington, D.C. es muy divertido. En la ciudad hay muchos eventos como la búsqueda de los huevos de Pascua en la Casa Blanca. Cada primavera miles de niños visitan la Casa Blanca para buscar huevos de Pascua.

Kids Enjoy the Easter Egg Roll at the White House

Los niños disfrutan de la búsqueda de huevos de Pascua en la Casa Blanca

The Capitol in Washington, D.C., is where members of the U.S. government meet to make laws. The building was finished in 1826.

El Capitolio, en Washington, D.C., es donde los miembros del gobierno de E.U.A. se reúnen para hacer las leyes. El edificio fue terminado en 1826.

The U.S. Capitol

El Capitolio de E.U.A.

Activity:
Let's Draw the Flag of the District of Columbia

Actividad:
Dibujemos la bandera del Distrito de Columbia

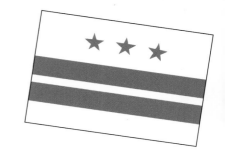

1

Begin drawing the flag with a rectangle.

Comienza a dibujar la bandera trazando un rectángulo.

2

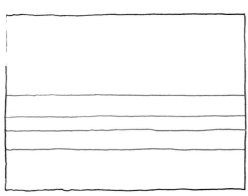

Add four horizontal lines. These will be the flag's stripes.

Agrega cuatro líneas horizontales. Estas serán las barras de la bandera.

3

Add three five-pointed stars in the center of the area above the stripes.

Añade tres estrellas de cinco puntas en el centro del área que está encima de las barras.

4

Erase extra lines inside the stars.

Borra las líneas extra dentro de las estrellas.

5

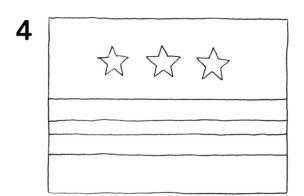

Color the stars and stripes. Great work!

Colorea las estrellas y las barras. ¡Muy bien!

Timeline | Cronología

Timeline	Year	Cronología
Congress decides that Federal City will be built on the border of Maryland and Virginia.	1789	El Congreso decide que la Ciudad Federal se construya en la frontera entre Maryland y Virginia.
Federal City becomes the U.S. capital	1800	La Ciudad Federal se convierte en la capital de E.U.A.
Federal City is renamed Washington City in honor of George Washington.	1801	La Ciudad Federal cambia su nombre en honor a George Washington.
British troops attack the President's House and the Capitol.	1814	Las tropas británicas atacan la Casa del Presidente y el Capitolio.
President Abraham Lincoln is shot in Ford's Theater.	1865	El presidente Abraham Lincoln es baleado en el Teatro Ford.
Martin Luther King Jr. delivers his famous "I have a dream" speech at the National Mall.	1963	Martin Luther King pronuncia su famoso discurso: "Tengo un sueño", en el National Mall.
The Pentagon is partly destroyed in a terrorist attack.	2001	Un sector del Pentágono es destruído por un ataque terrorista.

Events

January
Martin Luther King Jr. Birthday, 15

February
Chinese New Year Parade
George Washington's Birthday Parade

March
Smithsonian Kite Festival
Annual White House Easter Egg Roll

April
National Cherry Blossom Festival

May
Memorial Day Jazz Festival

June
Dance Africa
Hispanic-Latino Festival (All summer)

September
International Children's Festival

October
Columbus Day Parade, 12

December
National Christmas Tree Lighting

Eventos

Enero
Cumpleaños de Martin Luther King, 15

Febrero
Desfile del año nuevo chino
Desfile del cumpleaños de George Washington

Marzo
Festival smithsoniano de la cometa
Búsqueda anual de huevos de Pascua en la Casa Blanca

Abril
Festival del pimpollo del cerezo

Mayo
Festival de jazz del Día de los Caídos

Junio
Danza África
Festival hispano-latino (todo el verano)

Septiembre
Día internacional del niño

Octubre
Desfile del día de Colón, 12

Diciembre
Encendido de las luces del árbol nacional de Navidad

Distric of Columbia Facts
Datos sobre el Distrito de Columbia

Population
572,000

Población
572,000

Founding Date
1800

Fecha de fundación
1800

Motto
Justice to all

Lema
Justicia para todos

Flower
American beauty
rose

Flor
Rosa "belleza
americana"

Bird
Wood thrush

Ave
Tordo de la madera

Nickname
Capital City

Mote
Ciudad capital

Tree
Scarlet oak

Árbol
Roble rojo

Song
"The Star-Spangled
Banner"

Canción
"Barras y estrellas"

Famous People
Personajes famosos

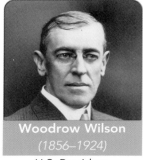

Woodrow Wilson
(1856–1924)

U.S. President
Presidente de E.U.A.

Duke Ellington
(1899–1974)

Jazz musician
Músico de jazz

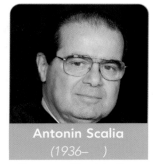

Antonin Scalia
(1936–   )

Supreme Court justice
Juez de la Corte Suprema

Marvin Gaye
(1939–1984)

Singer and songwriter
Cantante y compositor

Jesse Jackson
(1941–   )

Political activist
Activista político

Goldie Hawn
(1945–   )

Actor
Actriz

Words to Know/Palabras que debes saber

border
frontera

Congress
Congreso

slavery
esclavitud

Supreme Court
Corte Suprema

Here are more books to read about the District of Columbia:
Otros libros que puedes leer sobre el Distrito de Columbia:

In English/En inglés:

Washington, D.C
America the Beautiful Series
by R. Conrad Stein, Deborah
Children's Press, 1999

Washington, D.C
Rookie Read-About Geography
by Ribke, Simone T.
Children's Press, 2004

Words in English: 319   Palabras en español: 342

Index

Índice